Little, Brown and Company

Hachette Book Group
237 Park Avenue, New York, NY 10017
Visit our website at www.lb-kids.com

Little, Brown and Company is a division of Hachette Book Group, Inc.
The Little, Brown name and logo are trademarks of Hachette Book Group, Inc.

The publisher is not responsible for websites (or their content) that are not owned by the publisher.

First Edition: May 2013
Dracula vs. Grampa at the Monster Truck Spectacular and *Grampa's Zombie BBQ* first published in July 2006 by Little, Brown and Company
Monster Fish Frenzy first published in October 2006 by Little, Brown and Company

Library of Congress Control Number: 2012953634

ISBN 978-0-316-22850-3

10 9 8 7 6 5 4 3

RRD-C

Printed in the United States of America

Book design by Saho Fujii

The illustrations for this book were done in Staedtler ink on Canson Marker paper, then digitized with Adobe Photoshop for color and shade.
The text was set in Humana Sans Light and the display type was hand-lettered.

WRITTEN AND ILLUSTRATED BY

KIRK SCROGGS

LB

LITTLE, BROWN AND COMPANY
New York Boston

CONTENTS

AT THE MONSTER TRUCK SPECTACULAR

CHAPTERS

CHAPTER 1

It Takes Guts!

Ladies and gentlemen, boys, girls, dogs, and upper marsupials . . . the story I'm about to tell you is so frightening that I can't recommend it to the faint of heart, pregnant mothers, children under 46" tall, or the easily spooked. If you're scared of bats, rats, or old hippies, then this tale is definitely not for you.

So turn the page if you think you've got the guts. Otherwise, **BEWARE**! Children, grab your mammas! Elderly, take your heart medication! Prepare yourselves for the ultimate in raw terror. . . .

Don't get scared yet! That's not a monster. It's just Grampa. And that goop in his hand? Those aren't the brains of some poor kid....

Those are pumpkin guts. You see, it was Halloween night and Grampa was having his annual jack-o'-lantern carving contest. That's me, Wiley, next to Grampa and over there, that's Merle the cat torturing a june bug.

"WILEY, MY BOY!" said Grampa, pausing to put on a record. "The secret to an expertly carved pumpkin is to set the proper atmosphere. For tonight's listening pleasure I have selected "The Sound of Mucus" followed by "Old MacDonald Had One Arm and Ninety-nine Buckets of Blood on the Wall."

"Two of my favorites!" I replied.

Alas, it was my turn to gut the next victim.

"YUCK!" I grimaced as the stringy orange goop squished between my fingers.

"Kinda looks like one of your Gramma's casseroles, huh?" Grampa joked.

"I HEARD THAT!" yelled Gramma from the kitchen. "There'll be no Halloween snack treats for you if you keep that up!"

Gramma's casseroles may taste like pumpkin innards, but her Halloween snack treats are *par excellence* (that's French for "pretty darn good"). My favorite is her Screaming Skull popcorn balls with marshmallow brains inside.

SUGAR
GooP
MARSHMALLOW

At the awards ceremony, my one-eyed pirate was a hit, and Merle the cat presented a simple yet effective piece. Of course, we were no match for Grampa, whose carving of a Mediterranean village clutched first prize—not surprising since he was also the only judge!

"I call it *Pompeii Before the Eruption*," bragged Grampa.

"Show off," I muttered.

CHAPTER 2

Just Kickin' It

Next on the agenda was some serious rest and relaxation. Grampa and I kicked back, turned on the tube, and snacked on some black cherry soda and Pork Cracklins (that's deep-fried pig skin in layman's terms).

"OLD MAN!" yelled Gramma from the kitchen. "You better not get any pork crumbs on my new chair!"

"IT'S ALL RIGHT, GRANNY!" Grampa replied. "Merle's licking them off the upholstery!"

"SHHHHHH!" I shushed. "*The All-Night Mega Monster Scare-a-thon* is about to begin!"

"Good evening, kiddos! I'm Claud Bones, your horrible horror host! On tonight's menu we have three tasty tales of terror: *Dracula Down Under, The Nebraska Weed Whacker Nightmare,* and *Mayonnaise: The Motion Picture*! So turn out the lights, pop some corn, and prepare for utter terror! Tonight's flicks are brought to you by Velvet Knuckles hand lotion. For smooth skin that smells like honeysuckle, it's gotta be Velvet Knuckles."

The Dracula flick started off with a bang. A beautiful girl was sprawled on a sofa as a fanged creature of the night approached. He hovered above her, ready to chomp, and then...

some guy who's had too many chili dogs comes on chuggin' a bottle of Pepty Bizmo.

"It never fails," complained Grampa. "Just when it's getting good they gotta cut to a Pepty Bizmo commercial! It's just disgust—"

CHAPTER 3

A Dream Come True

That's when it happened! A TV commercial so awesome it stopped Grampa in mid-gripe.

"Tonight only!" shouted a crazed announcer. "The Gingham County Colosseum presents **Colonel Dracula's Monster Truck Spectacular**! Witness over 200 monster vehicles, including the world's only vampire truck! With special musical guest eight-year-old country sensation Lil' Buckaroo and the Texaflo Supreme Unleaded Dancers! Tickets are still available!"

We stared at the TV, trembling.
Pork bits fell from our mouths.

"World's only vampire truck,"
I said.

"Texaflo
Supreme Unleaded,"
Grampa drooled.

"Meow,"
meowed Merle.

But our bliss was
short-lived.

CHAPTER 4

Shattered Dreams

Channel 5's smarmy weatherman interrupted, "Hi, folks! Blue Norther here! I hate to ruin any trick-or-treat plans, but Channel 5's Whopper Doppler Radar has picked up an F5 tornado in the vicinity and if you've seen *Robo-Shark Vs. Lava-Twister*, you know that's a big one! So stay indoors, stay tuned to me, don't do anything fun whatsoever, and have a wonderful evening!"

“Grampa,” I pleaded, “we’ve just gotta get to that truck show! I don’t care if there is an F5 tornado!”

“Wiley,” Grampa replied, “there are more dangerous things than an F5 tornado.”

“Like what?”

“Like your Gramma if she finds out we’re going to a monster truck show in the middle of an F5 tornado!”

But it was too late. Gramma stepped in saying, "Don't you two get any harebrained ideas about going to that truck show! Didn't you hear Blue Norther? There's foul weather afoot!"

Now, Gramma's known to have a temper. You see that thing on her head? That's her anger meter, and the needle in Gramma's anger meter was starting to move into the red zone – a zone you *don't* wanna visit!

Grampa was torn. Sure, the idea of ridiculously souped-up monster vehicles destroying one another was hard to resist.

But was it worth risking certain death by tornado and flood?

Or, even worse, the wrath of Gramma?

I was sure Grampa would make the right and responsible decision.

So he lied to Gramma and told her we were going outside to check on the hounds.

"BE BACK IN TWO HOURS!" Grampa yelled back. Gramma looked pretty, pretty miffed.

Outside, the wind was picking up and thunder rumbled. The storm was approaching! Grampa's two hounds, Esther and Chavez, were already well prepared.

CHAPTER 5

The Trek

On our trek to the colosseum, we saw Nate Farkle trick-or-treating with his kids.

"Storm's coming!" he warned Grampa. "Blue Norther says there could be an F5 tornado, and if you've seen *Robo-Shark Vs. Lava-Twister*, you know that's a big one!"

“I’ve napped through F5 tornadoes!” Grampa bragged.

Grampa has been known to exaggerate, but I can verify that he *did* nap through the Great Septic Tank Explosion of 1999.

"Wiley," said Grampa, "if we wanna make it to the truck show in time, we're gonna have to cut through those woods."

"You mean those dark, scary, wild animal-infested woods?" I asked nervously.

"Why, that's the best kind, my boy!"

CHAPTER 6

The Woods

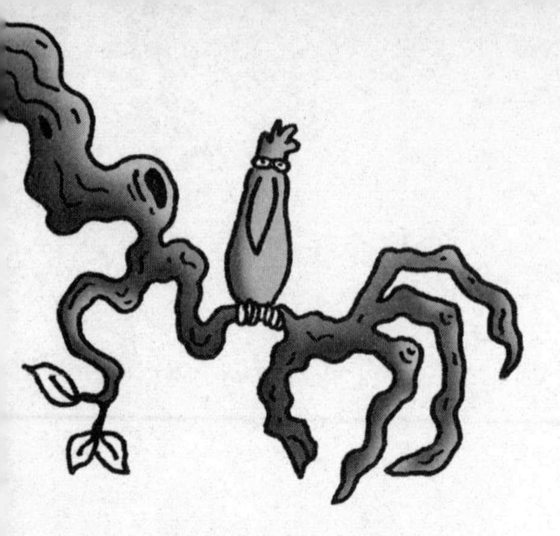

"You see those things up there that look like gnarled skeleton hands reaching out for you?" asked Grampa. "Well, don't worry. They're just tree branches."

"And those slimy things moving down around your feet? Don't worry. Those are probably just snakes looking for someplace warm, like your pants leg, to curl up for the night."

"Thanks for the words of comfort," I said.

"Don't look so worried, Wiley. Everything's gonna be just fine!" said Grampa.

Boy, was he wrong.

Lightning flashed!

The wind wailed!

Golf ball-sized hail
pounded my head!

Grampa napped!

CHAPTER 7

The Gingham County Colosseum

Finally, we crawled out from the woods — muddy, wet, and itchy. There before us was the Gingham County Colosseum — at least, I think it was the Gingham County Colosseum. Something about it just didn't seem right.

Inside, the place was a madhouse, stuffed to the brim with freaky people.

"Grampa," I said, "all these fans look pretty weird."

"It's Halloween, Wiley!" said Grampa. "Everyone's wearing costumes... or just really ugly."

Colonel Dracula stepped out in a black suede cape and plaid shirt and greeted the crowd in a funny accent.

"Velcome to the show, my vonderful friends! Tonight you vill see the most terrifying trucks ever to prowl the streets of Gingham County! But first, let me introduce our opening act!"

That's when Drac, accompanied by the Texaflo Supreme Unleaded Dancers, broke into a showstopping rendition of the disco classic "I Vill Survive."

"I think Drac should just stick to monster trucks," complained Grampa.

Finally, Drac brought out the vehicles. "This is gonna be good!" declared Grampa as the trucks hit the floor.

There was the **Behemoth Broncosaurus!**

Vlad, the Impala!

The **Invisible Van**, though it wasn't much to look at.

Even a **Werewolf Winnebago**!

"And now, ladies and gentlemen, I present my finest creation," said Dracula. "The **Mudsucker**! The vorld's first and only vampire truck!

"Ten liter, eighteen cylinders, all-veel drive, moon-roof, twenty-five disc CD changer vith detachable front, and six cup holders! And best of all — it drives itself! It took twelve mad scientists and twenty-three hunchback assistants over a century to create this baby!"

"Now," continued Drac, "I'll need two volunteers from the audience to help demonstrate the awesome appetite of the Mudsucker!"

"You hear that, Wiley?" said Grampa. "Raise your hand, quick!"

"I am, I am," I said, frantically waving my hand, **"BUT THIS ISN'T FAIR! THAT KID'S GOT SIX ARMS!"**

But to our shock and delight, Dracula chose us!

"You, the delicious-looking young child and that leathery, bony old creature beside you. Come on down!"

"Who's he calling old?" complained Grampa.

The crowd cheered for us as we stepped out into the arena.

CHAPTER 8

Skip the Lobster

"And now, these brave fools vill get into this classic **British Mini Pip-squeak** and play the ultimate game of chicken vith my monster truck! The Mudsucker and our guests vill take off at opposite ends of the arena, jump these ramps, and collide head-on above this fiery pit of giant mechanical lobsters!"

"**BOY!**" said Grampa. "And to think we were just going to stay home and watch TV all night!"

"WAIT A MINUTE!" I shouted. "This sounds like suicide!"

"Nonsense, my dear boy," said Dracula quietly. "I guarantee it is all perfectly safe. This is all just an act. There is no danger vat–so–ever. Now, if you vould just sign these insurance papers and an organ donor policy before ve begin."

We suited up, got in the Mini Pip-squeak, and waited. The tension was unbearable, as was Grampa's underarm odor.

"Sorry," said Grampa, "jumping over flaming pits of robot shellfish makes me perspire!"

Suddenly, Drac gave the signal.

The Mudsucker took off like a surface-to-air missile launched from the molten core of an erupting volcano!

Grampa took off with all the fury of a riding lawn mower with three wheels and a broken muffler!

The Mudsucker reached the end of the ramp and launched into the air like a mighty metal bird!

Grampa drove over the edge, straight into the open claw of lobster numero uno!

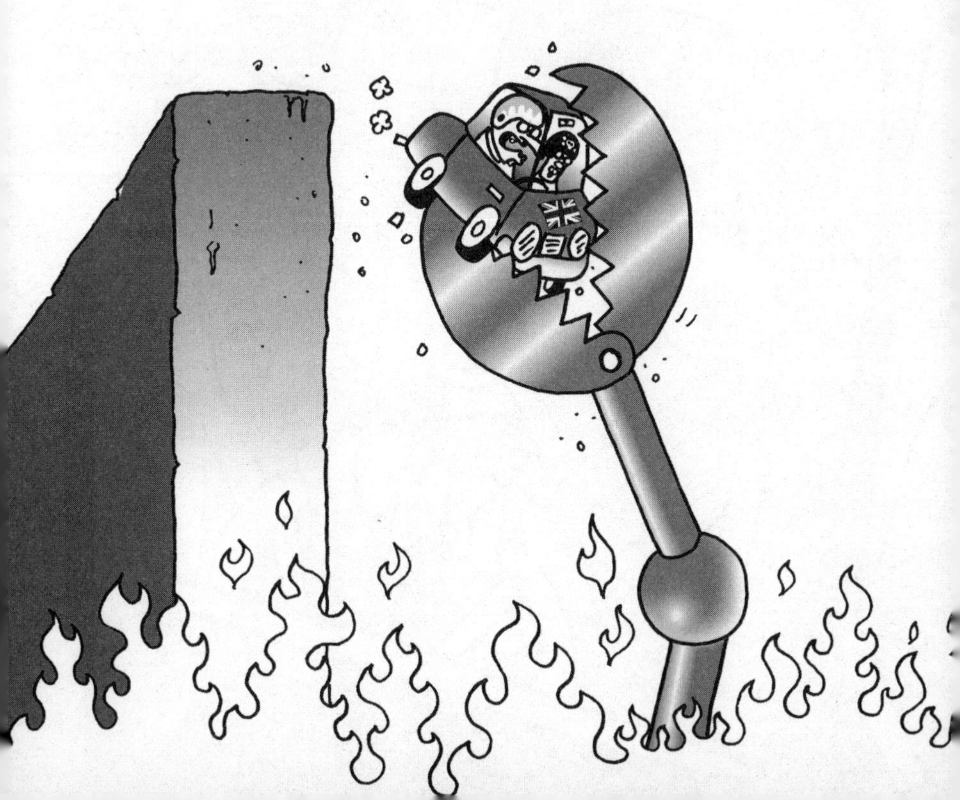

"WELL, THIS IS IT, WILEY!" said Grampa. "Snuffed out by a giant crustacean! I guess this is payback for all those seafood platters I've enjoyed over the years! If I'd only ordered the steak!"

But, lucky for us, the Mudsucker swooped in and clamped the lobster's claw with one of those lobster-clampy things. We heard a loud **CRACK!** and the lobster released our car from its deadly grip.

Then the Mudsucker caught us in its truck bed and, just for good measure, flung the metal lobster into a giant pot of boiling water.

"WHAT SHOWMANSHIP!" said Grampa as we coasted back down to the ground.

The crowd stood up and cheered as we exited the Mini Pip-squeak. I was never so glad to be back on solid ground.

"LET'S GIVE IT UP FOR OUR BRAVE VOLUNTEERS! VOO VOO VOO!" Drac yelled, pumping his fist into the air. "You see, I told you it vas completely safe."

"I knew it all along, Drac," said Grampa, trembling. "Now, if you don't mind, I'll be needing a heart specialist and a fresh pair of drawers!"

After the lobster incident, it was time for the halftime show with Lil' Buckaroo performing his country smash "Can I Get a Yeehaw?"

Grampa and I decided we'd rather chew on rusty barbed wire than listen to Lil' Buckaroo, so we headed for the snack bar.

CHAPTER 9

The Quest for Snacks

We waited in line at the snack bar while a rather shaggy gentleman purchased a big, hairy tarantula burger.

"I don't know much about truck show cuisine," I confessed, "but I've never seen tarantula burgers on a menu."

"It's not so strange, Wiley," said Grampa. "I ate a caterpillar cheese dog at the boat show just last April!"

Suddenly, I got the feeling that someone or something was looming over us.

Sure enough, Colonel Dracula was right behind us . . .

and he was staring at Grampa's wallet, mesmerized by the photo of Gramma standing in front of Grampa's 1956 Buick!

"Are you enjoying the show, my courageous lobster tamers?" Dracula asked.

"We sure are, Drac!" replied Grampa. "We braved rain, hail, and an angry Gramma just to see your tour de force of vehicular carnage!"

"Then perhaps you and the boy vould like a backstage tour vere you can meet the Mudsucker up close and personal?" Dracula offered.

"YOU BET VE VOULD!" exclaimed Grampa.

I wasn't so enthusiastic.

CHAPTER 10

Drac's Lair

Dracula took us deep into his cavernous lair.

"Please excuse the mess," he pleaded. "The maid vas eaten by a rabid porcupine."

Bats hovered above us. Spiders scurried below.

"VATCH YOUR STEP!" Dracula warned. "My piranha love the taste of small children."

"I HOPE YOU BROUGHT YOUR SWIM SUITS!" Drac said as we passed a rather uninviting swimming pool.

"No thanks, Drac," said Grampa, politely, "I always wait one hour after eating a tarantula burger before swimming or belly dancing!"

Drac's lair was most impressive. He had his own haunted library . . . a well-stocked, rat-infested wine cellar . . .

and even a plasma TV!

Past Drac's entertainment center and hanging above his hot tub was a strangely familiar portrait.

"LOOK, GRAMPA!" I shouted. "That picture looks just like Gramma!"

"Aaaah, yes," Drac said. "She vas my beautiful bride. She is no longer vith us. Dead for over vone hundred years! I'd rather not speak of her right now."

Drac got a little mushy and, I must admit, I got a little choked up myself. Tears were shed. Noses were blown. It was pretty disgusting.

All of a sudden, the lights went out!

"Grampa," I whined, **"I DON'T LIKE THIS!"**

"Don't worry, Wiley," replied Grampa. "There's gotta be a reasonable explanation for the power outage. Could be the storm, maybe Drac didn't pay his electric bill, or maybe a thousand angry rats have gnawed through the wiring and are heading toward us right now. It could be anything."

It was then that the lights came on again and Dracula was right behind us with the Mudsucker!

"BOY!" said Grampa. "This night is putting my pacemaker to the test!"

"Please," said Drac, "come closer and inspect my greatest invention! Don't be frightened. She von't bite!"

"She's a beauty, Drac! Let's pop the hood and see what this sucker's made of," Grampa said as he climbed onto the truck and peered into the engine. "Hey, Drac! Where is the carburetor in this baby?"

"It's underneath the tongue," Dracula said.

"OH YEAH!" Grampa replied. "There it is."

CHAPTER 11

Looking for Trouble

While Grampa drooled all over Drac's truck, I decided to do what all smart kids do in scary stories—go exploring by myself in the dark.

Drac's lair was bigger than I had ever imagined. I saw enormous parlors, ballrooms, and spooky crypts.

He even had escalators, pay phones, and fast-food joints. This place was impressive! In fact, I wasn't scared at all…

until, of course, I found Drac's collection of petrified skulls.

Then, to make matters worse, I backed right into Drac's assortment of non-friendly reptiles!

I quickly decided it was time to get back to the truck and find Grampa!

That's when I noticed that the Mudsucker was being refueled, but not with gasoline. It was being filled with, with . . . well, let's just say it's red and gushy and rhymes with **FLOOD!**

CHAPTER 12

Time to Go!

"OH MY, LOOK AT THE TIME!" I said, pushing Grampa toward the door. "We gotta be going!"

"Wiley," Grampa said angrily, "Drac was just about to show me his collection of ancient torture devices!"

"Trust me, Grampa," I said as we moved into the hallway, "we need to get as far away from this place as possible."

"Adios, Drac!" shouted Grampa. "We'll see you at the tractor pull next Thursday!"

As we made our way down the main hall, we heard a strange sound behind us. We stopped and turned to find the Mudsucker speeding toward us!

"Your Gramma never lets me drive the Buick in the house like that," complained Grampa.

"RUN!" I screamed.

And we ran...
through the corridors of the colosseum,
past the tarantula burger stand,
over Lil' Buckaroo...

We ran all the way to the exit, where
we found...

To our horror, there at the door was Gramma, and boy was she mad! Her anger meter was in the red, and we are talking redder than a sunburned lobster on a barn door!

"Well, Wiley, we made our beds and now we have to lie in 'em," said Grampa. "It's either the monster truck barreling toward us or the fiery anger of your Gramma. I'm seriously considering sticking with the truck."

But Grampa came to his senses and we quickly got into Gramma's car.

"HURRY, GRAMMA!" I pleaded.

"DON'T YOU HURRY ME!" she snapped back. "I'll teach you to lie to your..."

CHAPTER 13

Never Lie to Your Gramma!

Gramma's saucy tirade was cut short by the blinding headlights of the Mudsucker.

Dracula was right behind us!

"STEP ON IT, GRANNY!" yelled Grampa.

"CONSIDER IT STEPPED ON!" shrieked Gramma.

"MEOW!" meowed Merle.

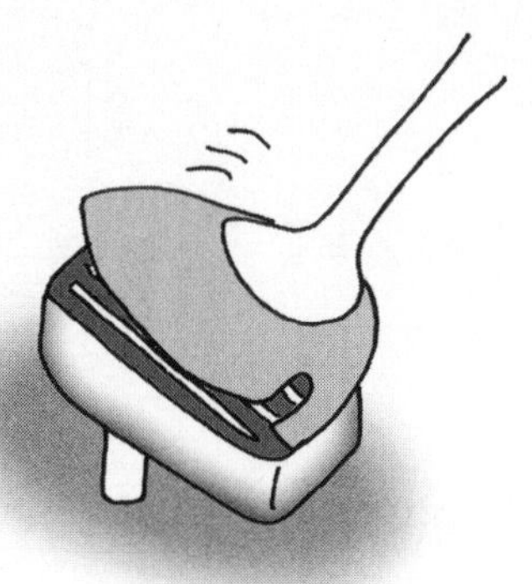

Gramma took off and hit warp speed in 6.5 seconds!

"**WILEY!**" Grampa yelped. "It's been nice knowing you! I only wish we could have lived to see that mayonnaise movie!"

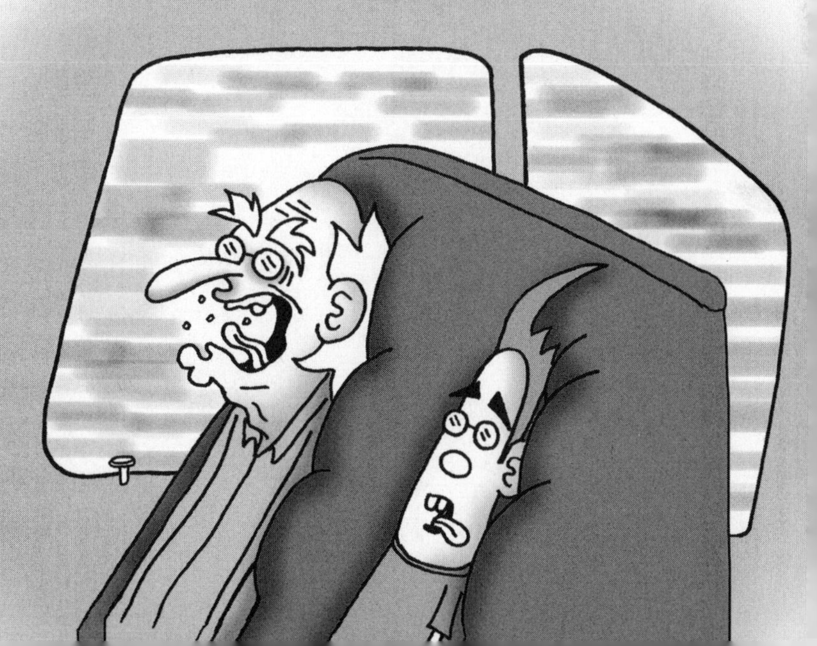

CHAPTER 14

It's a Twister! It's a Twister!

Gramma sped through the hills like a madwoman.

And wouldn't you know it? Right in front of us, blocking the road, was an F5 tornado! Blue Norther was right!

“Hold on to your drawers!” Gramma yelled. Then she did something that’s ill-advised (unless you’re being chased by a vampire truck) – she signaled and passed the twister on the left. It worked, too! We lost the Mudsucker! I gave Gramma and Merle the high five and Grampa...

Grampa was napping.

CHAPTER 15

Home Sweet . . . Uh-Oh!

At long last, we made it home. I shook Grampa awake.

"Eeeeyaaaa," he groggily yawned. "What'd I miss?"

"Just me saving your scrawny rear end from an F5 tornado," Gramma replied.

"Guess I napped through another one," he said as we pulled into the driveway to find…

AAAAAH!

Okay, now you should be scared. Dracula was waiting for us in the driveway with the Mudsucker at his side!

Grampa bravely jumped out and confronted Dracula.

"ALL RIGHT, DRAC!" Grampa challenged. "What do you want with my beloved family...and Gramma?"

Drac, sensing danger, assumed the famous Trembling One-Footed Bat stance!

Grampa, ready for the mother of all showdowns, struck his Crouching Cobra stance.

Gramma stuck to the more traditional Rumbling Shifty-Foot technique...

and Merle coughed up a mean hair ball!

I had to do something, so I valiantly jumped in.

"I know what you're up to, Drac! I saw how you looked at that photo of Gramma in Grampa's wallet, and I also got a good look at that portrait in your lair, which looks just like Gramma. Not to mention that you've been pumping that vampire truck with some pretty disgusting bodily fluids! It all points to one obvious conclusion!"

"It can't be too obvious," Grampa complained. "I'm terribly confused."

CHAPTER 16

Wiley's Theory

So I unveiled my theory: "Drac is after Gramma! She looks just like his long-dead wife. He wants to make Gramma his new vampire bride for all eternity!"

"OH MY!" said Gramma.

CHAPTER 17

Wiley's Theory Debunked

Dracula laughed, "No, no, no, my dear silly boy! Your Gramma is a lovely voman and she does resemble my dear dead vife, but it vas the **CAR** that I vas admiring in the photograph! I vant that 1956 Buick! I used to have vone just like it back in the day. Ahhhh, those vere the good old days. Riding around town, drinking black cherry soda vith my baby."

I must admit I felt a little bit foolish, but I was also extremely relieved.

Drac got a little teary eyed, and Grampa gave him a hug.

Even Merle and the Mudsucker made friends. Everyone was happy....

Except Gramma. She was a little disappointed.

CHAPTER 18

The Shady Transaction

Grampa happily sold Drac the Buick and even threw in a bag of Pork Cracklins.

"Drac, I gotta be honest," said Grampa, "this car breaks down about every other week and the weeks in between."

"It matters not," said Dracula. " I shall give it a complete tune-up and lube job, and then I vill replace the engine vith the heart of a Siberian volf hound!"

"Hey, whatever works," said Grampa.

Drac got so overjoyed with his new car that...

He turned into a bat!

"You people are so kind," Drac said, "and to think I vas considering draining the blood from your necks and feeding it to my truck."

"OH, YOU CHARMER!" Gramma said, blushing.

"**COME, MUDSUCKER!**" summoned Dracula. "You must return me to the colosseum before dawn!"

And they took off into the night.

"WHEW!" Grampa exclaimed. "Thank goodness! Storm's over! Sold the car! No harm done...."

CHAPTER 19

The Wrath of Gramma

A strange silence fell over us. Gramma was angry. In fact, Gramma's anger meter had moved from red to a new color never before seen by human eyes!

"What kind of grampa," she started, "drags his grandson through the woods in the middle of a tornado to see a truck show run by bloodsucking vampires?"

"But Gramma," I argued, "what kind of grampa would be **COOL** enough to drag his grandson through the woods in the middle of a tornado to see a truck show run by bloodsucking vampires?"

"The boy's gotta good point," said Grampa.

So that's my story, folks! As you can see, despite our night of unrelenting terror, everything turned out okay!

Grampa and I got home in time to see the explosive finale of *Mayonnaise: The Motion Picture.*

Gramma needed a new car, so Drac gave us a good price on the Invisible Van.

And Drac even joined Grampa and his buddies for Friday night poker. **(Grampa's poker tip #235**: Always let the vampire win!)

And as for the Mudsucker…

Let's just say, thanks to a deal I worked out with Drac, I had the coolest show-and-tell **ever!**

Gramma needs your super sleuthing skills to point out the differences between these two photos before she puts 'em in her wallet and shows them to her friends at the beauty parlor!

The answers are on the next page. No cheating!

CRACKPOT SNAPSHOT
SPOTTED BAT SYNDROME
MOTH KID
TALK TO THE BACK
RUDE TRUCK
HAT TRICK
SKELLY
MAMBA DOES MAMBO!
SNACK TRICK
HI-TECH DIMMER SWITCH
DIM
A HAIR DON'T!
A DIFFERENT TUNE
FUNKY COLD MEDEA
THE HAT ON THE CAT
FLIPFLOP
YIKES!
EYE CARUMBA!
JUST SHOE IT!

GRAMPA'S ZOMBIE BBQ
A TALE OF
UTTER TERROR...
GRILLED TO PERFECTION!
LITE-ER-UP
CHAR-COAL
ALL YOU CAN EAT!
SACK RACES AT 5:00

CHAPTERS

CHAPTER 1

Let's Do Lunch

Ladies and gentlemen, friends, neighbors, and out-of-town guests... since the dawn of time, zombies have captivated the imaginations of sick individuals all over the globe. From the voodoo rituals of Zambowi Island to the classic zombie movies like *Night of the Brain Munchers* and *Benji Conquers the Zombies*.

But there is one more zombie tale to be told. A tale so horrifying that your spine will tingle, your toes will curl up in their socks, and your nose hairs will wiggle uncontrollably. This is the story of **Grampa's Zombie BBQ!**

We begin our story with a scene from the classic zombie film *Fried Spleen & Tomatoes*.

No, wait! That's just Vera, the Gingham County Elementary School lunch lady, dishing up some of her world-famous* Bulgarian sausage and sourcrowt goulash. (*World famous for causing uncontrollable upchucking, that is.)

That's me, Wiley, about to dig into some seriously stinky cuisine. And that guy next to me is Jubal, my best friend in all of Gingham County—besides Grampa, of course.

"This cafeteria should be declared a federal disaster area," I said, staring at my plate of pulsating slop.

"And Vera should be brought to justice for crimes against humanity," added Jubal.

Some folks say she performs voodoo rituals on her three bean and cabbage chili!

Others say she uses genuine skunk meat in her spicy Indonesian wontons!

And noted physicians say that her kidney bean and oatmeal pasta with BBQ sauce is not carb friendly!

CHAPTER 2

The Big Announcement

"BARBECUE SAUCE!" I shouted. "That reminds me!" Then I stood up and made a very important and dramatic announcement: "Children of Gingham Elementary, I beseech you! Drop those sporks and put down those chocolate milks!

"You're all invited to my grampa's annual barbecue tomorrow at 2:22 PM!

"There'll be games, sporting events, cold beverages and, of course, my gramma's prizewinning honey paprika barbecue sauce! That's right—real edible food! Not this tub of guts they call goulash! Oh...and please, everyone, bring a covered dish, preferably mayonnaise free."

The cafeteria erupted in cheers. This was going to be the best barbecue ever!

CHAPTER 3

Kid Science

Later that evening at Grampa's house, Channel 5's smarmy weatherman, Blue Norther, went on about some solar eclipse.

"Hi, folks! Blue Norther here. We've just gotten word from the Gingham County Observatory that tomorrow at 4:44 PM, there will be a total solar eclipse! It will be an amazing sight only seen once every few years! Just make sure, whatever you do, that you don't look at it! Staring at an eclipse could cause blindness, glaucoma, cataracts, or your eyeballs could burst into flames!"

Normally, Jubal and I would rush to the TV at the mere mention of eyeballs bursting into flames, but we were too busy with our science homework. We carefully mixed various ingredients and compounds under the strict adult supervision of Grampa. . . .

Actually, Grampa was napping.

"And now, I shall add the final ingredient to my secret compound," I announced.

"Wiley, maybe you shouldn't add the Tabasco sauce!" Jubal warned. "I've got a bad feeling."

"NONSENSE, MY DEAR BOY!" I said defiantly. "What if Thomas Edison hadn't added the Tabasco sauce? We wouldn't have light bulbs today! What if Sir Isaac Newton hadn't added the Tabasco sauce?"

"No Fig Newtons?" asked Jubal.

"Precisely!" I said.

CHAPTER 4

Don't Try This at Home!

And if I hadn't added the Tabasco sauce...

that huge fireball wouldn't have shot over our heads...

soared across the room...

and landed on Grampa's unsuspecting foot, which went up in flames like a batch of dried twigs!

"HEY!" Grampa said groggily as he woke up. "What's that delicious aroma? Smells like bacon and blue cheese!"

"It's nothing, Grampa," I said nervously. "Go back to sleep."

Needless to say, Gramma was none too pleased. "I will not have dangerous chemical experiments in this house!" she bellowed. "What if that fireball had hit my new drapes instead of Grampa's foot?!"

Gramma forced us to dispose of our new compound, which I called PPK.

"It stands for Plutonium Powder Keg," I declared. "Jubal, we must hide this dangerous yet important formula where no human hands will touch it." So we hid it high on a shelf in the shed out in the backyard.

CHAPTER 5

Morning Marinade

The next morning at 6 AM, Gramma was already up trying out her new Super Marinade 5000.

"Wow, check out Gramma!" I said.

"I've got 375 chickens and 53 yards of sausage to marinade with my honey paprika barbecue sauce!" said Gramma as she hosed down the chickens. "That's the secret to my barbecue – lots of paprika! – Paprika, paprika, paprika!"

While Gramma prepared the poultry, Merle and I tested out the Slick 'n' Slide to make sure it was at the proper slickness.

Then I helped Grampa fire up the behemoth George Porkin Megagrill XE, which Grampa ignited by remote control, for fear of singeing his other foot.

"OOOOOH! I ALMOST FORGOT!" yelled Gramma. "Don't forget to make the lemonade!"

"IT'S ALL RIGHT, GRANNY!" said Grampa. "Merle's mixin' it as we speak!"

CHAPTER 6

Party Time!

By 2:30 PM, most of the guests had arrived and the party was hoppin'.

The delicious smell of BBQ brought visitors in from all over Gingham County.

At 3:00 we held our usual Watermelon Seed Spitting Championship. Gramma finds this quite disgusting.

Then it was time for Extreme Horseshoe Tossing.

At 4:00 we had our annual Gingham County Deaf Jam Poetry Reading (my least favorite BBQ activity).

And at 4:44 the local branch of Heck's Angels were in the middle of a mean game of volleyball with the Sisters of No Mercy when…

CHAPTER 7

There Goes the Sun

Suddenly, the sky went dark as an ominous shadow covered the sun. It was the eclipse! Blue Norther was right!

"OH, FIDDLE!" complained Gramma, sporting her new swimsuit. "I was ready to tan!"

"Well, this stinks," I said. "Maybe today isn't such a good day for a barbecue."

"Never fear, Wiley," said Grampa. "A little electromagnetic interference won't ruin our party. Besides, what else could go wrong?"

He had to ask.

Vera, the lunch lady, showed up with 27 gallons of her spicy beet borscht (that's ice-cold beet soup, for the uninformed). Everyone gasped and youngsters hid under the picnic tables.

"STOP!" I said. "Halt! Alto! I'm sorry. No further guests are permitted on the property! We have reached capacity. Besides, that borscht is considered a toxic substance by the League of Human Decency!" (I have to admit, I made that last bit up.)

"But...you said everyone who brought a covered dish was invited," said Vera, softly shedding a solitary tear.

"AND HE MEANT IT!" interrupted Grampa. "Of course you're invited! Wiley, where are your manners? Get this poor woman some refreshments and go put this borscht in the garage with the other dangerous chemicals!"

CHAPTER 8

Uninvited Guests

Just when things couldn't get any worse, Old Man Copperthwaite, the crazy gravedigger, came running and screaming like a banshee, "They're a comin'! The zombies are a comin'! They popped out of their graves and they're headed this way! Hundreds of 'em!"

"Hundreds of them?" said Gramma. "I hope they bring covered dishes!"

Sure enough, all of the residents of Eternal Naps Cemetery were crawling out of their graves and coming down the hill!

A virtual army of the undead was heading our way, and they sure looked hungry.

"DON'T PANIC!" Grampa assured the guests. "Everyone stay calm! There is nothing to fear! Zombies are people, just like you and me... except, of course, they've returned from the grave to eat our vital organs and perhaps gnaw on our bones a bit and maybe chew on our toes like jellybeans... but other than that, there is nothing to fear!"

The zombies got closer and closer, drooling and licking their rotten chops.

Our guests were getting nervous and I had to prevent a panic.

"DON'T WORRY, FOLKS!" I shouted. "We have guard hounds! They'll protect us!"

But Esther and Chavez were already bunkered in.

CHAPTER 9

The Not-So-Final Showdown

"OH, WELL!" I shouted, pulling out my slingshot. "It's up to us to fight the zombie menace! Citizens of Gingham County, arm yourselves!"

Gramma whipped out her kitchen arsenal.

The nuns struck their Praying Mantis stance.

Grampa napped!

The zombies slowly lumbered in and attacked!

"Oh, I can't stand it!" Jubal cried, covering his face with his hands. "The crunching of bones! The munching and smacking sounds of zombies eating our friends and neighbors! Oh, the humanity!"

"Wait a minute," I interrupted, "you can stop your wimpering, Jubal! The zombies are eating the barbecue! They must have smelled Gramma's delicious honey paprika sauce!"

"I'LL BE!" said Gramma.

"Wow, Granny!" exclaimed Grampa. "Your cooking usually sends people to their graves, not the other way around!"

CHAPTER 10

How to Entertain Zombies

So the zombies ate chicken and sausage and ate and ate, as fast as Grampa could grill. "Grampa," I said, " this is shaping up to be the weirdest barbecue ever!"

"You know you're right, Wiley," agreed Grampa, "even weirder than the Great Sack Race Collision of 1987!"

And things just got weirder....

Jubal got into a doozy of a tetherball match with Julius R. Gingham, our town founder, who had unsuccessfully wrestled a rabid coyote in 1862.

Gramma shared beauty secrets with the Ladies' Quilting League, lost in the Great Blizzard of 1912.

No BBQ would be complete without zombie karaoke (earplugs recommended).

And we held what had to be the world's first zombie sack race!

"These zombies may not talk much," said Grampa, "but they're courteous and gracious guests. Who would've thought that we'd be dining with legendary cowboy Wild Bill Hiccup and his wife?"

Grampa was right. Most people would think eating with a zombie would be pretty disgusting, but that just wasn't the case...

except for when Wild Bill's nose fell into the potato salad.

CHAPTER 11

A Vord of Varning!

"Ze zombie's appetite can never be satisfied!" came an eerie voice from the inflatable pool. It was Dr. Hans Lotion and his grandson, Jurgen. "Zey vill eat and eat and ven zey run out of food, zey vill eat vatever zey can get zeir zombie hands on! Zey vill eat anything!"

"Anything?" I asked, a little worried.

"Vell, almost anyzing," said Hans. "You know ze little vite chunks in ze pork 'n' beans? Even zombies vill not eat zat."

"So why have they returned from the grave?" asked Gramma.

"Could be anyzing," said Hans. "Ze Solar eclipse, global varming, ze smell of your delicious honey paprika sauce. Ve may never know. Vat I do know is zis, ve must appease ze zombies' appetites or suffer grave consequences!"

CHAPTER 12

Uh-Oh Part I

Nate Farkles made a poorly timed announcement at that moment. "Sorry, folks. We're out of barbecue!"

An eerie silence fell over the party as the zombies stared at us, drooling. "Be very still, Wiley," Grampa whispered. "Whatever you do, don't make any moves that might seem hostile or appetizing in any way."

CHAPTER 13

Total Chaos

Then the zombies went berserk and attacked the side dishes!

They devoured all 92 pounds of potato salad…

gnawed their way through forty-six ears of corn…

and wolfed down 54 pounds of baked beans, which created a whole new explosive situation!

TOOL SHE
PLEASE KNOCK BEFORE ENTERING
THE PARTY'S OVER

When the beans were gone, the zombies came after *us*!

"I don't want to alarm anyone," shouted Grampa, "but our gassy zombie guests are still hungry! Run for your lives!"

Some of the guests ran off into the woods.

The nuns, being natural climbers, headed for Grampa's big oak.

"LOOK, GRAMPA!" I shouted as we crowded into the house. "Heck's Angels are running away! Aren't bikers supposed to be tough?"

"I SHOULD HAVE KNOWN!" said Grampa. "Real bikers don't ride electric scooters!"

CHAPTER 14

Trapped!

Inside the house, we boarded everything up.

"LOOK!" said Gramma, pointing at the TV. "Blue Norther is about to make an emergency announcement!"

We all waited in hushed silence.

"Hi, folks! Blue Norther here at the 51st annual Betty Crockpot Bake-Off, where I'm standing with Minnie Purvis, the grand prize winner! Not only has Minnie brought us a sample of her delicious Baked Nebraska with butter-creme filling, but she's agreed to share the ingredients to this delicious dish with our viewers right now!"

"Zombies are attacking and that's his emergency news?" I griped.

"And they call this journalism," complained Grampa.

"I gotta write this down," said Gramma. "This is good stuff!"

Suddenly, the zombies casually strolled in through the back door, which had been left unlocked!

CHAPTER 15

Up Yonder!

"QUICK!" I yelled. "Everybody run upstairs, where there's absolutely no chance of escape!"

All twenty-seven of us piled into Grampa and Gramma's bedroom, and we blocked the door with Gramma's collection of romance novels.

"Well," announced Grampa, "that should keep them out for at least ten minutes!"

CHAPTER 16

The Blame Game

"Why is this happening?" asked our hysterical neighbor Loretta Cartwright. "Why are zombies roaming Gingham County?"

"It's the solar eclipse!" shouted old man Romero.

"I think it was something in that barbecue!" said Betty Hubris. Gramma found this statement particularly hurtful.

"NONSENSE!" I interrupted. "There is a perfectly logical reason for what's happened. It's all her fault! Vera, the lunch lady! The second she arrived, everything went haywire! She's evil… *evil!!!*"

"WILEY!" bellowed Gramma, her anger meter in the red. "I am ashamed of you! Don't you know it's not polite to blame the dead rising from their graves on a dinner guest?"

I must admit, I felt a little silly.

All of a sudden, a meow for help caught our attention and we rushed to the window!

"Oh no!" shouted Gramma. "Merle's trapped in the garden shed and the zombies are coming for him!"

CHAPTER 17

Dead Bug Walkin'!

Merle was securing his minicompound when an eerie buzz came from above. It was the bug zapper, glowing a ghastly blue.

To make matters worse, the dried dead bugs under the zapper were getting up and walking! And they were coming for Merle!

"Kitty! Kitty!" buzzed the dried bug zombies as they closed in on Merle for their cat dinner.

"OH, I CAN'T WATCH!" cried Gramma.

"Don't worry, Honey," comforted Grampa. "Just think of it this way, you'll never find another hairball in your fluffy slippers ever again!"

CHAPTER 18

To the Rescue

"I can't just sit back and watch!" I yelled bravely. "I've got a plan to rescue Merle! All I need is a pair of Gramma's finest and strongest panty hose!"

"I always knew that boy was talented!" said Grampa.

So Jubal and I grabbed a pair of Gramma's stockings and shimmied down to the shed while the hungry zombies clutched at our feet.

We burst into the shed to find... Merle had pulled the old reverse-bug-munch trick and was picking little hairy bug legs out of his teeth.

"MEEEOOOOWWWUURRRPPP!" said Merle. (That's cat for "Burp!")

"That's pretty sick," said Jubal.

CHAPTER 19

Secret Weapon

We were just about to escape the shed when I suddenly remembered our explosive compound up on the top shelf.

"I KNOW!" I shouted. "While we're down here, let's grab the PPK! Maybe we can use it against the zombies!"

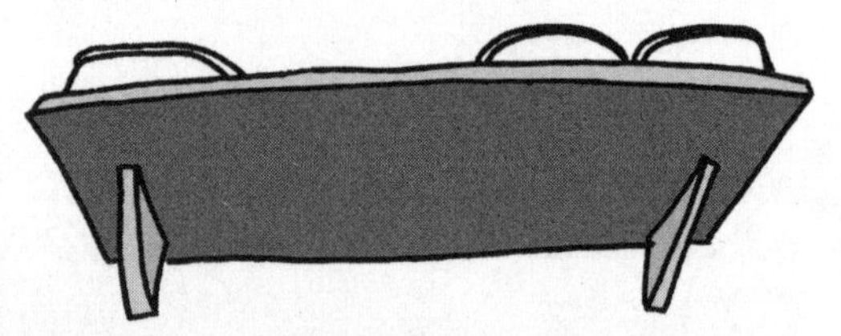

CHAPTER 20

Uh-Oh Part II

So we formed a human-feline ladder to boost me up to the shelf so I could grab the secret…

"HEY! IT'S GONE!" I yelled. "All I see up here is a bunch of paprika!"

Paprika? Suddenly, I had a very, very bad feeling.

My mind raced as I recalled the events leading up to the zombie attack.

"I shall call it PPK!"

"I'll put it high on the shelf where no human hands will get to it!"

"That's the secret to my barbecue!—Lots of paprika!—**Paprika, paprika, paprika!**"

"UH-OH!" I said gloomily.

So we shimmied back up to the bedroom to deliver the bad news.

"Boy," I said, panting, "this is a lot harder going up!"

"I wish I hadn't eaten five plates of barbecue!" complained Jubal.

Gramma was so happy to be reunited with Merle that she gave him a big bear hug.

"Careful, Granny," warned Grampa, "that cat's already survived one near-death experience!"

CHAPTER 21

An Embarrassing Confession

"Ladies and gentlemen," I announced, "I'm afraid I have an embarrassing confession to make...."

"That's a good idea, Wiley," Grampa interrupted. "Because we soon will most likely be devoured by zombies, I too have something I'd like to get off my chest. Something that now, in our final moments, I have come to terms with: I am a life-time member of the Pippi Longstocking Fan Club. I also bite my toenails and sleep with a teddy bear named Shmuggles."

CHAPTER 22

Not That Embarrassing!

"No, no, no," I broke in, "Jubal and I have done something horrible! We created a chemical compound so powerful it blew up Grampa's foot! And that's not all! We accidentally hid the compound on Gramma's spice rack in the shed!"

"What are you saying?" asked Gramma.

"I'm saying that our compound made its way into your barbecue sauce and that could be the reason why its delicious aroma woke the dead!"

Gramma went off like Mount Krakatoa! "You mean to tell me," she fumed, "that because of you, I put a highly volatile chemical in my beloved barbecue... one that explodes–"

"THAT'S IT!" I interrupted her tirade. "Our compound explodes when combined with Tabasco sauce! If we could douse the zombies with the stuff, we could blow 'em up! But where do we get enough Tabasco?"

"My spicy beet borscht is 82 percent Tabasco," offered Vera the lunch lady, "but you locked it in the garage."

I was so happy I could have kissed her (but I didn't). "We've got to get to that borscht!" I exclaimed. "If only we had something we could distract the zombies with to get to the garage!"

"I've got just the thing," said Grampa as he pushed a button on his universal remote. Just then, Gramma's portrait of Elvis opened up to reveal a monster stash of Pork Cracklins!

"Succulent deep-fried pig skins to distract the zombies!"

"Why would you need this many Pork Cracklins?" asked Gramma, still angry.

"In case of World War III," said Grampa, embarrassed, "or a pork shortage."

CHAPTER 23

The Plan Comes Together

So I laid out my plan. "Grampa and I will use the Pork Cracklins to draw the zombies away from the house!"

"Meanwhile, Jubal and Nate will disguise themselves as zombies and make their way to the garage, grab the borscht, and then we'll dump it on the zombies!"

Gramma and her Ladies' Quilting League friends knitted us suits made out of Pork Cracklins.

Grampa and I squeezed in a power workout to beef up for our dangerous mission.

The Reverend Moe said a prayer for us. "Protect these crazy fools. And if they are caught by the zombies, let their deaths be quick and relatively painless!"

Finally, we used Gramma's avocado and cucumber face mask to turn Jubal and Nate into zombies.

We were ready. The game was afoot!

CHAPTER 24

The Not-So-Great Escape

Grampa and I burst into the crowded hallway in our Pork Cracklins suits. We quickly ran for the stairs.

"COME AND GET IT, YOU FILTHY ZOMBIE SWINE!" yelled Grampa. "All you can eat grampa and grandson! The boy tastes just like chicken, and I taste like aged angus beef! And did I mention, we're covered in pork rinds?"

While Grampa taunted the zombies, Jubal and Nate snuck out and silently slipped in with the zombies, unnoticed.

"Yuck!" grimaced Jubal, dripping with avocado face cream. "This stuff is gross!"

"I kinda like it," exclaimed Nate. "My pores are tingling and my skin has never felt so young!"

Grampa and I made it out the front door and took off across the yard. But the zombies were gaining on us!

Just as the zombies were about to catch us, we made it to the Slick 'n' Slide and slid out of their rotten zombie grasps. (It should be noted that zombies are notoriously afraid of open flame, the metric system, and Slick 'n' Slides.)

"OH, NO!" I screamed, looking back toward the house.

"Jubal and Nate are aborting the mission!"

It seemed that the zombies had smelled the avocado face cream and were chasing Jubal and Nate with tortilla chips.

"Sorry, guys!" yelled Nate. "Who knew zombies were partial to guacamole?"

"We've got to get braver friends," complained Grampa.

CHAPTER 25

Uh-Oh Part III

We turned and tried to escape, but we ran smack dab into Gramma's cactus garden. There was nowhere to go. We were trapped like Pork Cracklin–covered rats.

"Well," said Grampa as the zombies closed in on us, "this is it, Wiley. The end of the road! I only wish we could have lived long enough to eat these suits!"

CHAPTER 26

It's Raining Borscht!

"HEY, ZOMBIES!" yelled a voice from the hill. It was Gramma. Apparently, while the zombies were chasing us, she had slipped out the back and grabbed her Super Marinade 5000 . . . and better yet, she had filled it with Vera's borscht!

"Soup's on!" Gramma yelled as she hosed the zombies down with the toxic borscht.

"Just beet it!" she remarked as she slathered more of our undead guests.

"How 'bout another serving?" she remarked as she sprayed the last of the zombies.

And, just as I had predicted, the zombies reacted explosively with the borscht and ran away, which was good because Gramma was almost out of borscht *and* witty one-liners.

CHAPTER 27

Adios!

The zombies, outwitted by beet soup and Pork Cracklins, ran back home to the cemetery.

"And next year, don't show up unless you're invited!" yelled Gramma.

"You know, Wiley," said Grampa, "if it weren't for the awful stench and the fact that they tried to eat us, those zombies wouldn't be half bad! I think I might invite them back for spaghetti night!"

CHAPTER 28

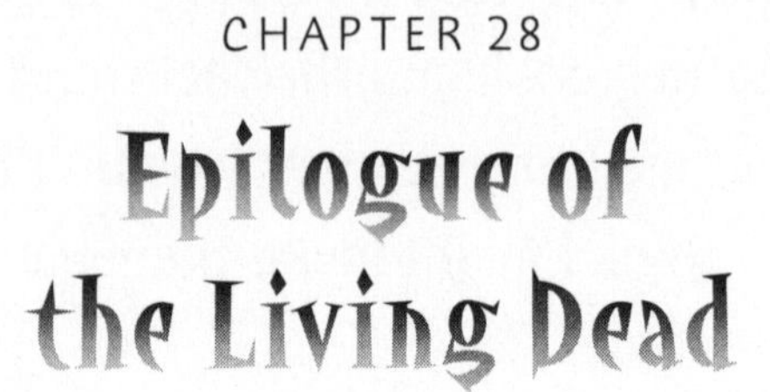

So that's my story, folks! Everything turned out peachy keen. Gramma and Vera were declared heroes.

Vera's borscht was purchased by the government for study and possible military use.

Gramma's story was turned into a hit action movie.

As for our secret compound, Jubal and I decided to bury it in a secure location…

deep in the woods, where it could cause no further harm to humanity.

Oh well,
at least we tried.
PET SEMETERY
SCRATCH 1961-1970 RABIES
PISCO
HERE LIES WIGGLES
CUJO THE TURTLE
FANGS
SCOOPY POOP
BUTCH 1972-1983 WORLD'S MEANEST PIT BULL
NEMO

What's up with Jubal's camera? He took two shots of the Zombie Karaoke Sing-Off, but there's something about the second picture that just doesn't seem right. Can you pick out the differences between the two pictures, or are we just crazy?

The answers are on the next page. Anyone caught cheating will be fed to the zombies with a tangy honey mustard sauce!

CRACKPOT SNAPSHOT
GINGHAM COUNTY IDOL
GIANT AMOEBA TRAPPED IN A BALLOON!
QUITE A STIR
DO THE MASH POTATO
EYE POPPING!
SNAC MAN
SPEAK INTO THE DRUM-STICK
SCARY CHEST
LETS BOOGIE!
COOL CAT
BUCKLE UP
WHAT'S UP, DOC?
DEATH METAL
JITTER BUGS
ALLIGATOR BOOTS

MONSTER FISH FRENZY
DEEP-FRIED
TERROR AWAITS!
EVEN RUDER

CHAPTERS

CHAPTER 1

Sounds Fishy to Me

Ladies and Gentlemen, you are about to encounter a species of fish thought to be extinct for 65 million years—Big Bassosaurus Rex. It weighs approximately 6 tons. That's 2,650,003 fish sticks for all you less-educated people out there. If you meet up with this fish, do not make any sudden movements, and whatever you do, never call it cruel names like Blubber Butt or Big Lips Pooperstink! Proceed with extreme caution!

Don't get scared yet! That's not the bloated, bloodshot eye of a monster kid-eating fish!

That's just Paco, Grampa's prize pet goldfish. And that's me, Wiley, filming Grampa and Paco for *America's Most Talented Animals*.

"Please observe," I said quietly, "as Grampa feeds Paco his favorite cuisine, Pork Cracklins."

Paco's even crazier for Pork Cracklins than Grampa is. In fact, he can detect Cracklins from miles away and he'll do anything for those succulent pork bits.

He can leap through sizzling beer-battered onion rings.

He can play dead.

He even does a mean Elvis!

"I wish you two wouldn't go on about that fish!" complained Gramma. "You're gonna upset Merle! After all, he's a talented animal, too. Just look at him!"

"You're right, Granny," said Grampa. "But he's no match for this fish. Paco's gonna make us so rich we'll blow our noses on $100 bills! The world will be our oyster!"

"Oyster!" I shouted, interrupting Grampa's loony rambling. "I almost forgot! It's All-You-Can-Eat Fried Oyster & Waffle Night at the Crustacean Plantation! We've only got two hours left!"

CHAPTER 2

Tentacle Lickin' Good

Crustacean Plantation, Gingham County's swankiest seafood restaurant, was filled to the brim with satisfied diners.

We were met at the door by Captain Gerald, the one-handed owner of the restaurant.

"Ahoy there!" said Captain Gerald. "You fine folks sit right down and make yerselves at home while we stuff your bellies with the finest deep-fried marine critters this side of the Gulf of Mexico!"

The food was squidliscious! Gramma and I got started on the oysters and waffles while Grampa had an octopus salad with zesty ranch dressing.

"Hey, that reminds me," I said. "In school today, we learned that a sea cucumber is the only creature that can spit up its internal organs and then grow new ones."

"Wiley!" said Gramma, shocked and sickened. "Not while we're eating!"

"Yeah!" said Grampa, a ranch-drenched tentacle hanging out of his mouth. "What are you trying to do? Gross us out?"

"Can I get ye some more fried oysters and waffles?" asked Captain Gerald.

"Ye sure can," I said, "with extra syrup!"

"Shiver me timbers!" said Captain Gerald. "I haven't seen an appetite like yours since the fish that swallowed me hand!"

I was intrigued. "You mean..."

"Moby Fizz!" gasped everyone in the restaurant at the same time.

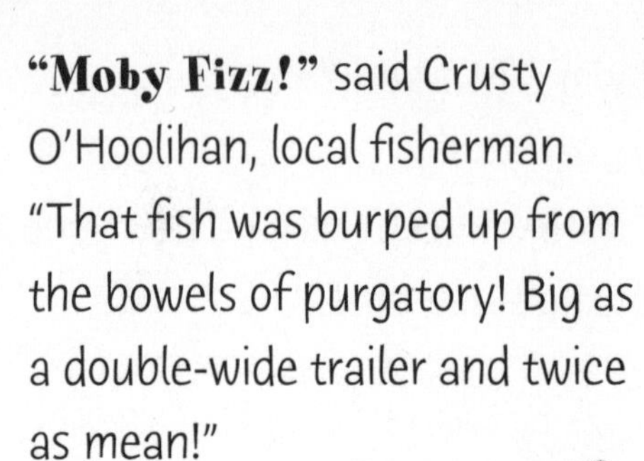

"Moby Fizz!" said Crusty O'Hoolihan, local fisherman. "That fish was burped up from the bowels of purgatory! Big as a double-wide trailer and twice as mean!"

"That cursed fish ate my pet poodle, Dinky!" said Marjorie Millner, local old person. "He went out for a dog paddle and I never saw him again!"

"Aaay!" continued Captain Gerald. "One minute I'm synchronized swimming with the boys, the next, I'm in the hospital with one hand missin'. There's only one man who's laid eyes on Moby Fizz and still has all of his limbs. In fact...

he's sitting right there!"

"What, what?" Grampa said, jolted out of his nap. "Is it time for dessert?"

"We wanna hear about Moby Fizz!" I said.

"Moby Fizz! Moby Fizz! Moby Fizz!" we all chanted, banging our maple-syrup dispensers on the table.

"All right! All right!" Grampa said. "The tale I'm about to tell you is so secret and personal that I've never told it to anyone other than all my friends and family at every social gathering for the last seventy-five years."

CHAPTER 3

The Tail of Moby Fizz

"It all started many, many years ago when I was a tiny ragamuffin, no taller than a bag of grain. Today, you know me as Grampa, but back then, people called me Ishmael."

"I thought they called you Little Stinker," said Gramma.

"Don't interrupt me, Granny," said Grampa. "Call me Ishmael."

"One day, I decided to prove my manhood and embark on a solo fishing voyage. Just me and the open water... and my favorite stuffed animal, Captain Froggy, of course. We set out on a little wooden dinghy into the heart of Lake Putrid. The swells were about 5 feet, the wind was at 10 knots, and my hair was looking particularly stylish.

"Everything was going wonderfully...

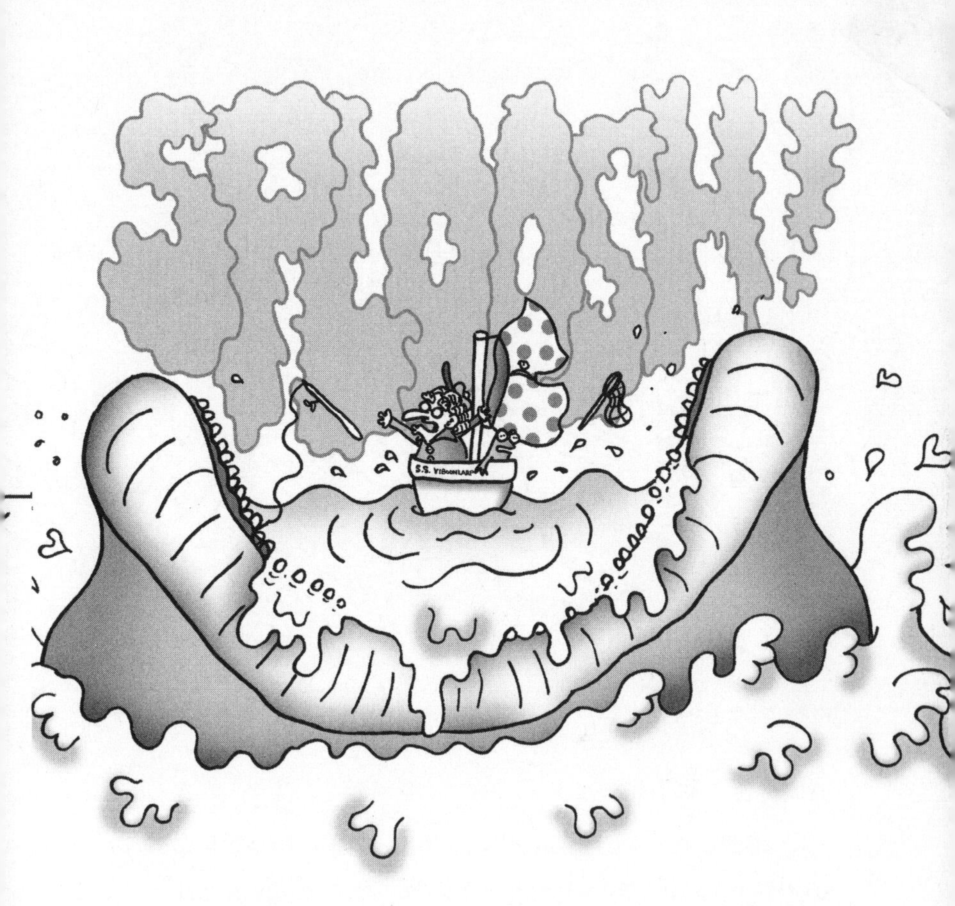

that is, until we were attacked by the biggest, most bloated, most deformed bass the world has ever known! In one gulp it swallowed us up—boat, frog—the whole enchilada!

"So there we were, stuck inside of a monster fish with the million other things he had swallowed.

'Well, this is it, Captain Froggy,' I said. 'We're done for! Doomed to be digested in a fish's gut for all eternity! This is sure gonna look silly on our tombstones.'

"Lucky for us, Moby had swallowed a shipment of carbonated, fizzy water on its way to a circus-clown colony on the North Shore. I shook every one of those bottles of fizzy water until they exploded, filling the air in Moby's stomach with carbon dioxide gas. Pretty soon the fish started to bloat and rumble until…

Moby Fizz let out the biggest release of natural gas since The Great Texas Chili Cook-Off of 1907! The burp blew me clear out over Lake Putrid.

"But Captain Froggy didn't make it. He was caught on Moby's teeth like a piece of spinach. Those blubbery fish lips closed on Froggy and he slipped down beneath the waves never to be seen again.

"I floated for days until I was rescued by the Gingham County female waterskiing team, the Ladies of the Lake. A small, round girl about my age carried my withered, little body as we skied back to shore.

"And that," concluded Grampa, "was the first time I laid eyes on Gramma and we began our life together, which is another tale of terror entirely that we don't have time to get into right now."

The crowd was stunned by Grampa's story.

"Death to Moby Fizz!" screamed Crusty O'Hoolihan.

"Avenge my poodle!" demanded Marjorie Millner.

"Where are my waffles?!" shouted a disgruntled diner.

"Aaaay!" said Captain Gerald. "Let's have ourselves a little contest! I'll offer a king's bounty to whoever finds Moby Fizz! Dead or alive or deep-fried—let's go fishin'!"

CHAPTER 4

A Vord of Varning!

"Leave ze fish be," said a creepy voice. It was Dr. Hans Lotion and his grandson, Jurgen. "If you disturb zat fish, it vill bring grave misfortune on Gingham County. It vill eat your children as if zey vere tangy, chewy gummy bears!"

We all took Dr. Lotion's warning very seriously.

"Did I mention I'll throw in free all-you-can-eat fried oysters and waffles?" said Captain Gerald.

The next day, everyone in town showed up at Lake Putrid to hunt Moby Fizz. My best friend, Jubal, joined our team and Gramma packed us some of her world-famous pimento and cheese sandwiches.

"Pimento and cheese! Thanks, Granny," said Grampa. "We can use it to plug up any leaks should we start sinking!"

The contestants prepped their boats and checked their gear and fish weaponry.

Even Grampa's hounds, Esther and Chavez, got in on the action.

CHAPTER 5

Yo Ho Ho and a Bucket of Chum

Spirits were high as we set forth on our grand adventure! First, we did an equipment check.

Life jackets—check!

Assorted hooks, tackle, and slimy bait—check!

One vat of chum made from fish guts, rotten eggs, buttermilk, and horseradish—check!

"Um!" said Grampa, smacking his lips. "This chum's not half bad! Kinda tastes like one of your Gramma's power smoothies!"

"I heard that!" yelled Gramma from the shore.

"Grampa," I said, pulling out a rather scary-looking map...

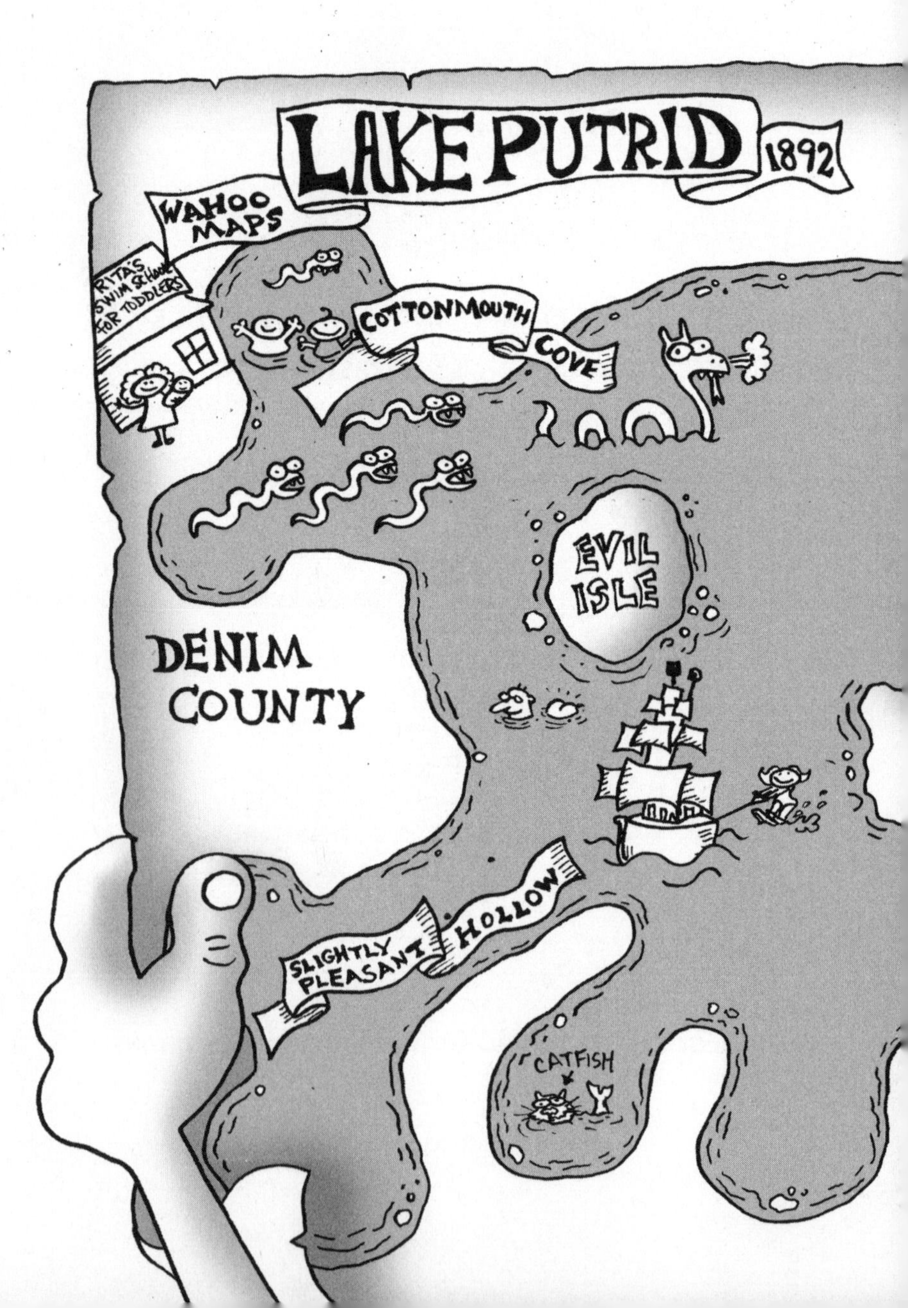

"before we get too far, there are some areas on this map of Lake Putrid that we should definitely avoid like..."

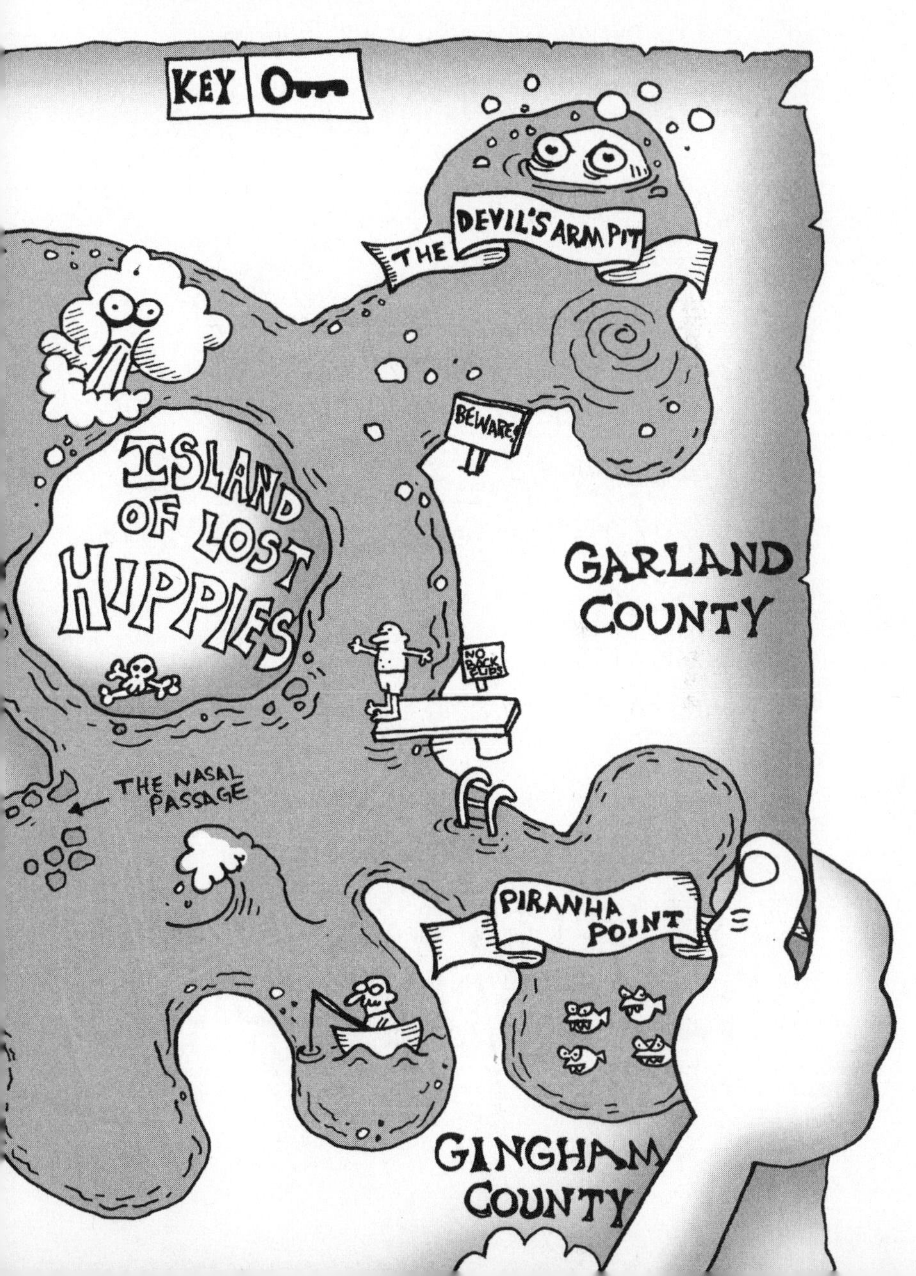

"Maps shmaps!" said Grampa. "I've been lost on this lake dozens of times for days on end and I never needed a map! Why, I can just sniff the wind and follow my nose and it will lead us straight to that stinky beast!"

So Grampa sniffed the wind and his nose led us straight to...

It was Vera, Gingham Elementary's world-renowned lunch lady and master food poisoner!

"What are you doing here?" I asked, horrified.

"Oh, hello, sweety!" Vera replied. "I'm just gathering algae and water bugs for Monday's lunch special. I call it Sweet and Sour Seafood Surprise."

"I gotta remember to pack my lunch," said Jubal.

Vera whipped out an electronic contraption. "I have to warn you boys. My Electromagnetic Radar Fish Detector thingy's picked up a large mass in these waters."

"Wow!" I said. "She's got an Electromagnetic Radar Fish Detector thingy!"

"You don't need a fancy gizmo to find Moby," said Grampa. "Ever since my little fizzy water incident, Moby's been gassier than an Exxon station. All you gotta do is watch for the bubbles. If you see bubbles, you got troubles!"

CHAPTER 6

Bubble Trouble

All of a sudden, the water churned with bubbles and Moby Fizz surfaced beneath Vera! Moby stared at us with an eye as big as a trampoline.

“We’re gonna need a bigger boat,” I said.

“And a lot of tartar sauce!” added Jubal.

CHAPTER 7

Piranha Point

As quickly as he had appeared, Moby swam away. But Vera had been knocked overboard!

"Holy mackerel!" I shouted, pulling out my map. "If my calculations are correct, we're in Piranha Point! Legend has it that a disgruntled pet store employee released a piranha in this cove years ago and now the place is teeming with them! We've got to get her out of the water! A school of piranha can devour a water buffalo in sixty-five seconds!"

"Wow!" said Jubal. "It takes me at least ten minutes!"

"That piranha business is just an old wives' tale!" said Grampa. "Look, I'll put my hand in the water and nothing will happen!"

"Okay," said Grampa, "maybe swimming isn't such a good idea!"

Unfortunately, a school of piranha had already homed in on Vera's splashing and was heading her way!

"We've got to do something!" shouted Jubal.

He was right. I had to act fast.

So I pushed Jubal into the lake!

"Hey, piranha!" I shouted. "Come over here! Eat my friend instead! He's got a lot more meat on his bones and he's low in polysaturated fats!"

The school of piranha fell for it and changed course. Now they were heading directly toward Jubal!

At the last minute, just as the little beasties were about to sink their teeth into Jubal's soft hide, I tossed one of Gramma's pimento and cheese sandwiches into the lake.

The piranha went for the sandwich while Jubal and Vera climbed onboard. Everyone was safe and sound.

Except for the piranha. They didn't survive the pimento and cheese sandwich.

"I'll never underestimate the power of your Gramma's cooking again," said Grampa.

"I heard that!" yelled Gramma from the shore.

CHAPTER 8

Tail of Destruction

"Toodles!" said Vera as we departed. "Thanks for rescuing me! I'm gonna make you a special dish for lunch on Monday!"

"You shouldn't!" I yelled back. "Really, you shouldn't!"

As we headed deeper into Lake Putrid, we saw that Moby Fizz had left a trail of total devastation. The other contestants and their boats were in shambles!

We floated up to Nate Farkles, clinging to all that was left of his boat—his prize collection of ceramic penguins.

"I don't know what happened," said Nate. "All I did was throw a razor-sharp harpoon at Moby Fizz and he goes and destroys my boat!"

"Hang in there!" said Grampa. "Help is on the way! I wish we could help, but this boat's reached maximum weight capacity. Besides, I've got a monster fish to find and a stuffed frog to avenge!"

CHAPTER 9

As the Worm Turns

Moments later, we heard a sickening slurping noise.

"Stop the boat!" I said. "Shhhhhhh! Listen."

"It's Moby Fizz!" said Jubal. "He's found us!"

But the slurping seemed to be coming from the ice cooler, and it was getting louder and slurpier.

Grampa reached over slowly and pulled off the lid to find…

It was Merle, and he was slurping up earth-worms like fettuccine Alfredo!

"A stowaway!" exclaimed Grampa. "In the pirate days, this sneaky varmint would've had to walk the plank for this!"

"I don't think Gramma would like that," I said.

As time went by, Grampa became more and more determined to find Moby Fizz. He just wasn't himself. He got all whiskery and disheveled and wasn't gonna stop until he found that fish.

It was hard on us kids, too. The labor was back-breaking, the sun beat down on us with no mercy, food was scarce, and scurvy was setting in!

"I can't believe we've only been out here for two hours," said Jubal.

And as if things couldn't get any worse, Blue Norther, channel 5's smarmy weatherman, appeared on Grampa's portable combo T.V./radio/toaster/espresso maker.

"Hi, folks! Our Whopper Doppler radar's picked up a northern front from Iceland and this swirlylooking cloud thing from Peru. If these two systems collide it'll probably be real bad. So stay inside and stay off Lake Putrid! In the next few minutes, that lake will become a churning, swirling death trap! Have a wonderful day!"

"Grampa," I pleaded, "you heard Blue Norther. This dinky little boat can't withstand a thunderstorm, let alone a swirly cloud thing from Peru! Let's head back to shore!"

"Absolutely not!" said Grampa. "I'd brave a Gale 7 hurricane, a sea of burning oil, a swarm of killer bees…why, I'd even trim my nose hairs with a rusty Weedwacker before I'd give up Moby Fizz!"

"Wow! That's dedication," said Jubal.

CHAPTER 10

An Imperfect Storm

Blue Norther was right. The two storms collided directly over us just as we were entering the most dangerous part of Lake Putrid—The Devil's Armpit!

"Maybe we should put on our life jackets," I suggested.

"Don't be silly," said Grampa. "I've nearly drowned in storms dozens of times and I never needed a life jacket!"

CHAPTER 11

Take It from a Big Mouth

Before we knew it, we were face-to-face with the mother of all monster fish, Moby Fizz!

"Wiley!" Grampa bellowed. "Hold her steady! Jubal, prepare the net!"

"I don't think he's gonna fit in this net!" said Jubal.

"He will when I get through with him!" said Grampa, raising his harpoon.

But before Grampa could throw the harpoon—Whap! Moby used our little boat to practice his power serve! We were plunged into the icy depths of Lake Putrid.

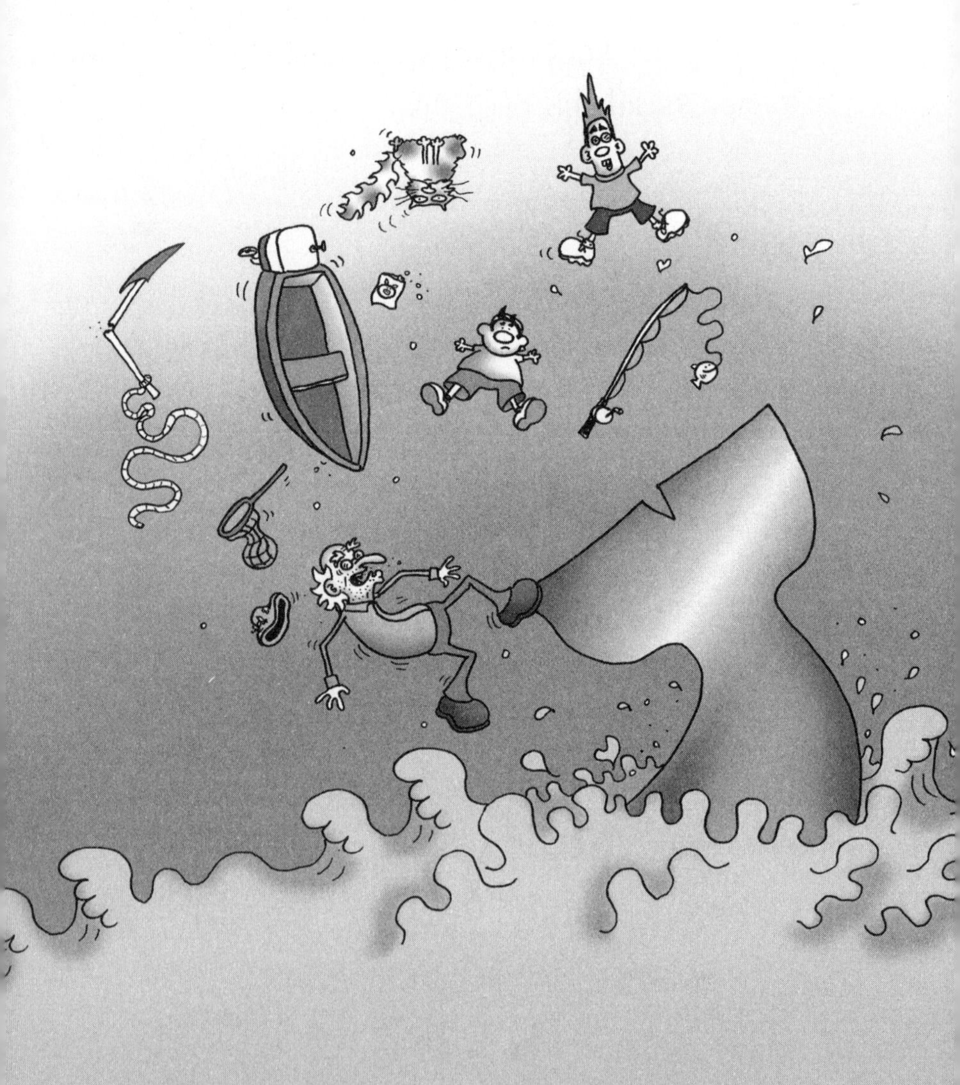

Beneath the water I was tossed around by the current like a pair of dirty drawers in a giant washing machine.

I was about to black out when I noticed something strange and horrifying—I could see Moby Fizz skimming the bottom of the lake and he was sporting a big, grotesque appendage that was sucking up fish by the hundreds. This thing truly was a monster!

CHAPTER 12

Captain's Log

I gathered my strength and swam to the surface, where I found the others floating on a stray log.

"Nice of you to join us, Wiley," said Grampa. "We were just kickin' it. Tellin' a few knock knock jokes."

After a while, the storm clouds cleared and the waters were calm again.

That is, until suddenly, the water around us began to churn with bubbles!

"Oh no!" I yelled. "The bubbles! Moby's back for seconds!"

"Actually, that was me," said Grampa. "I never should have had that second can of chili for breakfast."

So, Jubal, Merle, and I got our own log.

Soon, night fell and we drifted off to sleep. My slumber was troubled by nightmares and visions.

In my dreams I saw Grampa, transformed into a grizzled old Captain Ahab, obsessed with avenging Captain Froggy.

I saw Gramma desperately searching for her missing loved ones.

And I saw myself, ruling over a colony of tiny talking pickles who worshiped me like a Greek god. (This part has nothing to do with anything, but I thought it was pretty cool anyway.)

CHAPTER 13

The Island of Lost Hippies

We awoke to find ourselves in grass skirts, surrounded by smiling hippies!

"Don't worry, kids," said the head hippie. "Your clothes are drying by the fire."

"If I'd known I was going to be wearing a grass skirt in public, I would have hit the gym first," Jubal said, embarrassed.

"These things are pretty comfy," said Grampa, "and they're great for hula dancing!"

"Ughhh!" I groaned. The sight of Grampa in a skirt was just too much for my young eyes!

"You're on the Island of Lost Hippies," said a girl hippie known as Earth Mother. "Tall, short, round, skinny—we all wear grass skirts. No one should be ashamed...

except for Artie, of course.
I mean, that's just wrong."

So we gathered around the campfire in our skirts, and roasted marshmallows and drank root beer floats. Grampa entertained the hip-pies with the story of Moby Fizz.

Later that night I had a heart-to-heart with Earth Mother.

"Earth Mother," I said, "I'm worried about Grampa. He's not himself. He only thinks of catching Moby Fizz and nothing else."

"Your grampa is plagued by the past," she said. "Confront this mighty fish he must. Just look at him. He's been sitting on that cliff for hours, staring out at the open water, waiting for the moment he can take on the scaly beast and move on with his life."

Actually, Grampa was napping.

CHAPTER 14

Extreme Boat Makeover

In the morning, the hippies woke us with a surprise. They had found our boat and repaired it while we slept!

"First we sealed the leaks with tree sap and acorns," said the head hippie, "then we coated the entire boat with a protective layer of snail mucus."

"Then we added a 1,200 horsepower Liquijet 5000 jet-boat engine with a magnetron electronic ignition, outboard hydraulic tilt and trim, and a twist-grip throttle."

"Wow!" I said. "Where did you get that?"

"Oh, on the other side of the island," said Earth Mother. "There's a Manny's Boat World next to that veggie-burger joint."

After bidding a sad farewell to our new hippie friends, we took off once again in search of the elusive Moby Fizz.

"Look at those nutty hippies," said Grampa. "They're waving their hands, dancing around and screaming like crazy people. How cute."

CHAPTER 15

Big Mouth Strikes Again!

So we waved back and jetted off, straight into the open mouth of Moby Fizz!

At least, I thought it was Moby Fizz. The inside of the fish was all shiny and there were lights and signs and some soothing smooth jazz playing over a loudspeaker.

"Wow!" exclaimed Grampa. "They've really done a lot with this place! It used to be so... slimy."

"This isn't a real fish," I said. "It's some sort of—"

"Submersible android fish research vessel, to be exact!" said a familiar voice. It was Dr. Hans Lotion and his grandson, Jurgen. "I call it Robo-carp! You must forgive me for attacking you yesterday. Ze Robo-carp mistook you for an enemy threat."

"So what do you do on this tub of bolts, Doc?" asked Grampa.

"Come, I vill show you."

"Ze fish shape of zis vehicle allows us to conduct our studies vithout disturbing ze natural habitat of Lake Putrid," said Hans as he gave us a tour of the ship. We saw the mess hall, the Captain's quarters, the poop deck, you name it.

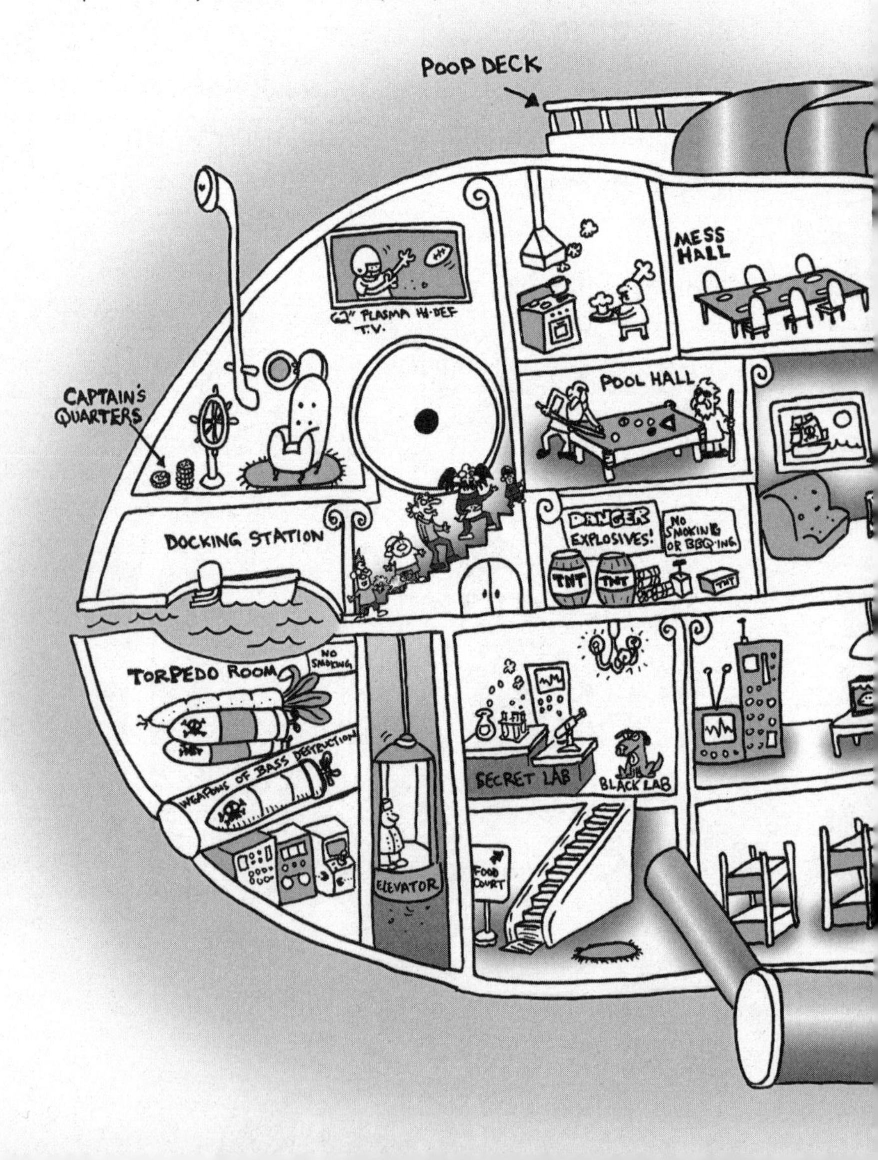

"Jubal," I whispered, "something about this smells funny."

"Are you sure it's not the poop deck?" asked Jubal.

"No," I said. "There's something about Hans I don't trust."

Hans showed us an impressive model of his vessel. "Ve all know zat pollution is ze biggest threat to our beloved lake right now.

"Robo-carp is equipped vith a retractable suction device zat vacuums ze pollution and scum from ze bottom of ze lake. I plan to clean up Lake Putrid vithin three months. I call my plan, Operation Scumsucker! I am also currently vorking on a giant scumsucking pig. Look for it in stores next Christmas."

Hans then showed us to our quarters. "In ze morning, ve vill return you to your vorried Gram-mam-ma. For now, rest. I must varn you—stay avay from ze engine room. Robo-carp runs on a top secret and dangerous energy source. In fact, do not leave your rooms. I vouldn't vant any mishaps."

CHAPTER 16

A Pleasant Development

We took Hans's warning very seriously and immediately decided to go exploring. Robo-carp was enormous. There were doors and hallways everywhere.

"Let's try that door right there," said Grampa, "the one that says 'Go Away!' on it."

So we went inside and found…

Hans had the biggest fish tank I've ever seen and in it must have been almost every fish in Lake Putrid!

"Something's not right!" I said.

Then I found Hans's blueprints for a new, swanky development called Lake Pleasant.

"I think I've figured it out!" I said. "Hans is digging his fancy new Lake Pleasant while he scares everyone away from Lake Putrid with this phony monster bass and steals all of the fish with that scumsucking vacuum attachment. Hans is just a lying, greedy, evil fishnapper!"

"Well, nobody's perfect," said Grampa.

"Vell, Vell, vell!" said Hans. "I vas going to invite you to play Parcheezy and instead, I find you've been snooping around! Yes, it's true. Lake Pleasant vill be ze new vacation destination in Gingham County and ze tourists vill spend all zeir money in my hotels, restaurants, and doggy day cares. Lake Putrid vill dry up and die. Vhat good is a fishless, polluted lake haunted by a monster bass?

"Now I have to decide vhat to do vith you. Torture perhaps? Maybe... termination?"

"My vote's for Parcheezy!" said Grampa.

CHAPTER 17

Hanging Around Fish Organs

Before we knew it, we were hanging from the rafters in Hans's music room.

"Vhile my grandson beats you vith a piñata stick, I shall entertain you vith some organ music," said Hans maniacally. "Vhat vould you like to hear? Some disco? How 'bout 'Who Let Ze Dogs Out?' "

"All this time I thought Hans was just a good foot doctor," said Grampa. "Who knew he was such an accomplished psychopath?"

Suddenly, Hans's organ music was interrupted by a loud alarm. An unidentified object was approaching! Hans whipped out his periscope and scanned the horizon.

Meanwhile, Merle started to gnaw on our ropes.

"Zere is a triangle of large elderly vomen approaching!" said Hans.

"Sounds like your Gramma," said Grampa.

While Hans was distracted, Merle finished gnaw-ing through the ropes and we made our escape.

But first we had to make a stop and release the scaly citizens of Lake Putrid.

We found the escape hatch in the rear of the Robo-carp and we plopped into the lake.

"This is strangely degrading," said Jubal.

Just as we suspected, Gramma had come to the rescue and she was perched atop the reunited Gingham County female waterskiing team!

And boy, was she was angry! "I'm gonna teach that fish a lesson!" she bellowed as they sped toward the Robo-carp.

The robot fish readied its torpedoes, did a quick U-turn, and was heading straight for Gramma, when the unthinkable happened!

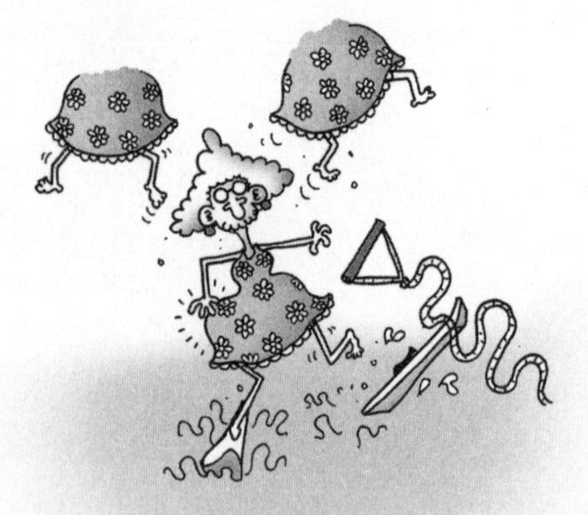

Cleta Van Snout's artificial hip suddenly gave out! The Ladies of the Lake went flying!

Gramma launched into the air like a mighty albatross!

Then she grabbed hold of a latch on the side of the fish.

Gramma accidentally moved the latch, opening up a large compartment. About 2,563 AA batteries spilled out into the lake!

"So that's Robo-carp's secret energy source," Grampa said, disappointed.

CHAPTER 18

Sayonara Robo-carp!

The clunky metal fish was powerless without its batteries, and it quickly capsized.

"You have not seen ze last of me!" shouted Hans as the Robo-carp sank. "I vill be back! And next time I'm bringing a giant metal chicken! Or perhaps a salamander!"

"How did you ever find us?" I asked Gramma.

Gramma held up Paco's fishbowl. "We used Paco to track your trail of Pork Cracklins all the way to that island full of nice hippies. They told us we could find you in the belly of a giant metal fish!"

"Wow!" I said. "A Cracklin-trackin' goldfish!"

"So I guess it was Hans's fish that has been scaring folks these last few years," I continued. "I wonder whatever happened to the real Moby Fizz?"

"I can't help but feel a little silly," said Grampa. "My crazed obsession with finding that fish put everyone in danger. Moby Fizz is just a faded memory, like tiny bubbles in a bottle of flat black-cherry soda."

Once again, the water around Grampa began to churn with bubbles.

"Let me guess," I said. "You had a third can of chili for lunch."

"Nope," said Grampa. "As much as I'd like to take credit for these bubbles, it wasn't me."

CHAPTER 19

Will the Real Moby Fizz Please Stand Up?

Suddenly, the real Moby Fizz surfaced beneath us, and let me tell you, after 60 million years, his breath was kickin'!

Grampa jumped onto the bloated beast and flailed away!

"This is for Captain Froggy!" he yelled as he smacked Moby with his bony arms.

The Ladies of the Lake struck back at Moby in their famous Swooping Falcon formation.

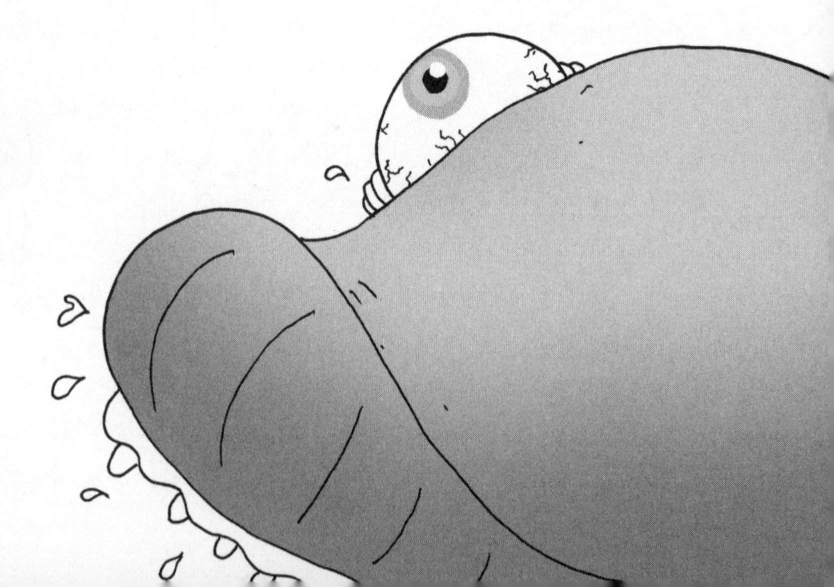

But the monster put up a fortified force field of fish breath that stopped them in their tracks.

Not even Merle's sofa-ripping cat claws could penetrate Moby's thick hide.

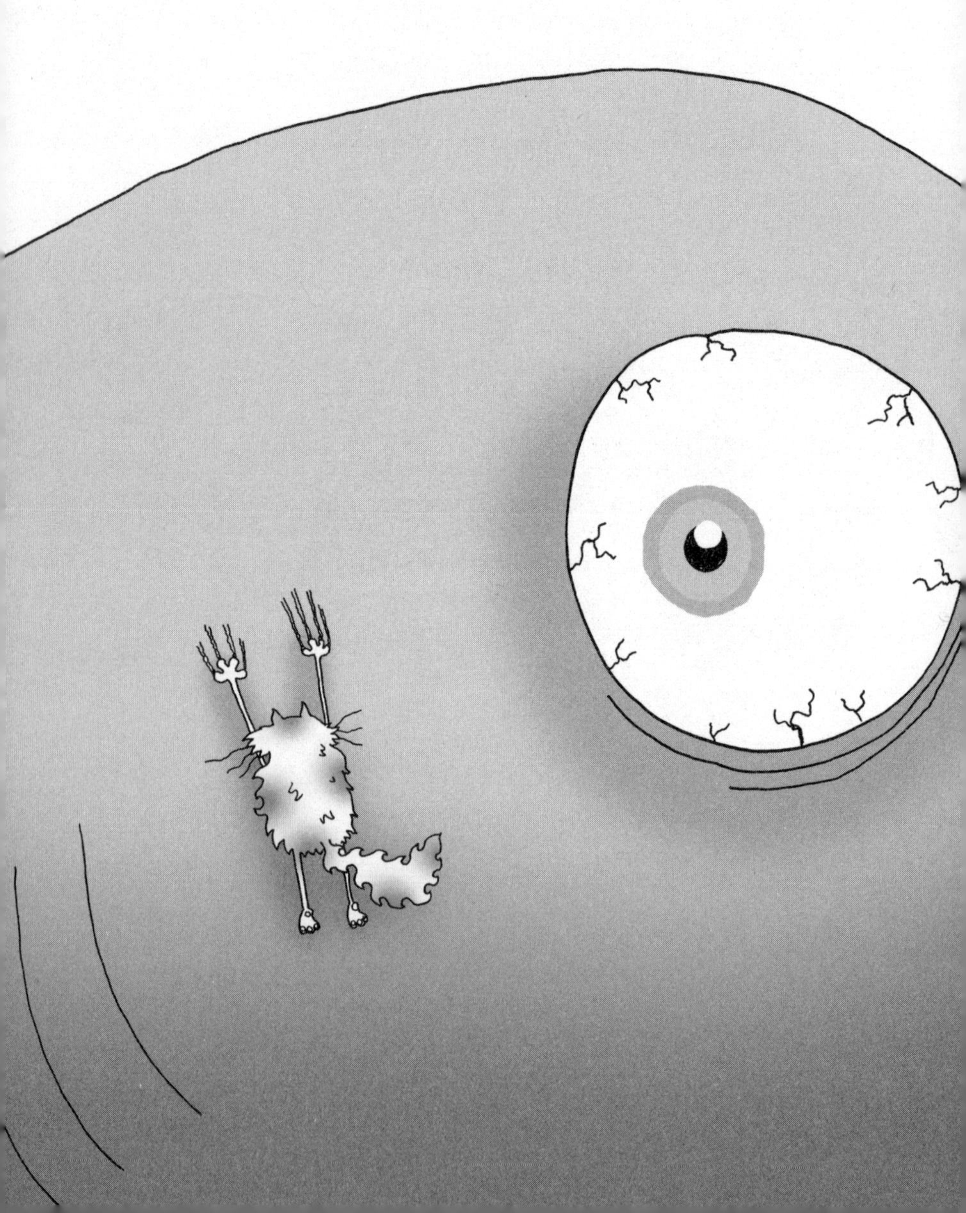

The fishy foe leaped into the air, and his mammoth body was going to crash directly on us!

"Well this it, boys," said Gramma. "I only wish I could've lived to yell at your Grampa for getting us into this mess!"

As a last resort, I held up Paco's fishbowl.

"You wouldn't harm a fellow fish, would you?" I pleaded.

That's when the strangest thing happened—Paco jumped up and communicated with Moby. It kinda sounded like a chipmunk on helium.

Whatever Paco said, it stopped Moby dead in his tracks. He got a sad look on his face, turned around, and swam away.

Moby resurfaced briefly and gently let out a tremendous fish burp. A mysterious object was dislodged by the burp and it flew straight toward us.

The object landed with a splat in Grampa's arms. It was Captain Froggy!

CHAPTER 20

Reunited and It Feels So Slimy

"Froggy!" Grampa shouted with glee. "My brave, little, green, fish mucus-covered friend!"

All was well with the world. Froggy was back in Grampa's arms, the Ladies of the Lake were back together, and the lake was putrid again.

"Let's all go home and put on some dry drawers!" shouted Grampa.

So, Moby Fizz wasn't the monster he was made out to be. Captain Gerald confessed, "So okay, my hand didn't get bitten off. I had a splinter that got infected, but that just doesn't sound as cool."

"What about my Dinky?" asked Marjorie Millner.

"Maybe Moby mistook your poodle for a cream puff or a wad of cotton candy when he ate him," said Grampa. "I know I've done it!"

Captain Froggy was placed on the mantel in the living room. Gramma found this highly disgusting.

And Hans and Jurgen were locked up at the Gingham County Institute for Criminal Masterminds and Their Grandchildren.

As for Paco…

Paco achieved his dream of competing in the finals on *America's Most Talented Animals*.

But, unfortunately, he faced some big competition.

Something's fishy about this family portrait! We got double prints at the local photo lab, but one of the pictures looks wacky. Help us figure out the differences.

The answers are on the next page. Anyone who cheats will walk the plank, sleep with the fishes, and mow the lawn!

CRACKPOT SNAPSHOT
YEE HAW!
UNARMED
CATCHING THE RED-EYE
PREHISTORIC FISH BREATH
WIPE-OUT!
TIC TAC D'OH!
14 CARRO
GOLD FILLING
STILL GASSY
COLD BEVERAGE
BABY CAT
BUG NAPPER
OUCH!
STILL ANGR
PIRANHA PACO
FLORAL PRINTS ARE IN
GET HAPPY
OL' NESSIE
HOT AIR IS OUT